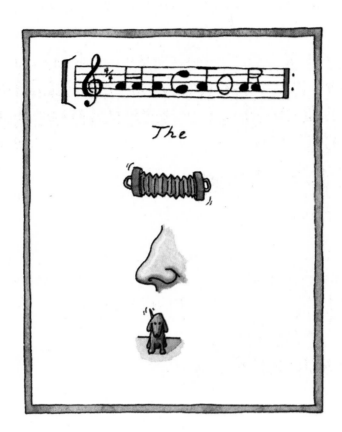

To Karin and Ellen
and to all the Baukhols of Vinstra, Norway

HECTOR

The Accordion-nosed Dog
by John Stadler

BRADBURY PRESS / SCARSDALE, NEW YORK

As a boy, Hector lived quietly in the mountains. But once at school, he was found to have an outstanding talent and his life began to change. At graduation, Professor Sludge presented him with the Peabody trophy, the highest honor for excellence in pointing.

Professor Sludge insisted that Hector demonstrate his pointing technique for the eager gathering of parents and teachers.

"Now watch his nose, folks," the professor said as Hector prepared himself.

Hector was all concentration. He tensed his body and sniffed the air. Suddenly, he pointed with his finger and nose to a fly on a rabbit's ear over one mile away.

"Perfect form!" called out one spectator.

"And how well he uses his nose," added another. Hector blushed.

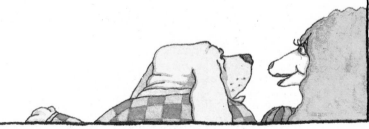

Competing in the Olympic Games, Hector won eleven gold medals. An all-time record!

"What form! What a nose!" the sportscasters said again and again.

Hector was an overnight sensation and his life became a whirlwind. He starred in several TV commercials, and even made a movie.

Hector moved into a spacious townhouse in the heart of the city.

"This is the life!" he said.

He was fast . . .

. . . and dashing . . .

. . . and everyone wanted to be his friend.

For a long time, Hector spent most nights at his favorite spot, dancing and prancing into the wee hours of the morning.

Early one dawn, as Hector was showing some admirers just how fast he could run, something terrible happened.

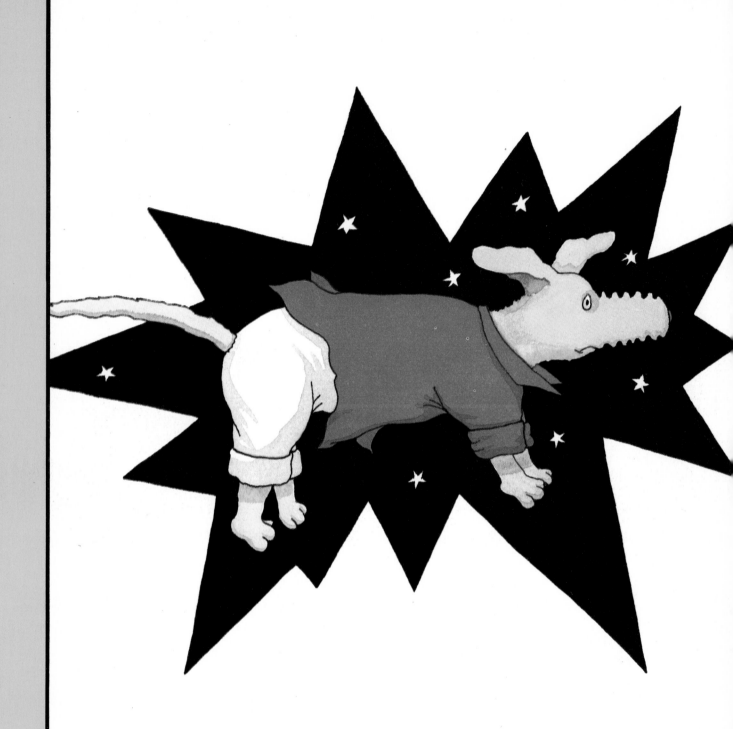

He ran squarely and soundly, smack into a wall.

Hector looked as stiff as a poker, but someone
called for a doctor, anyway.

When Hector finally awoke, he was lying in a
hospital room that was filled with strange music.
Realizing that he was still alive, he shrieked with joy.

"Now hold on there, Hector," the doctor shouted over the loud music. "You've made a remarkable recovery. However, I must tell you that your nose . . . er—well . . . it's turned into an accordion."

"Huh?" Hector said.

Following his release from the hospital, Hector, overwhelmed with despair, went for a walk along the shore.

"I'm finished," he moaned. "With such a weird nose, I'll never point again."

Back home Hector disconnected the phone and locked his door. He looked through old scrapbooks full of his past. From time to time he entertained himself with a tune on his bent, musical nose, but he never went out. Finally, Hector's landlord threw him out.

"You didn't pay your rent, buster," he yelled, "and besides—I hate your crummy music!"

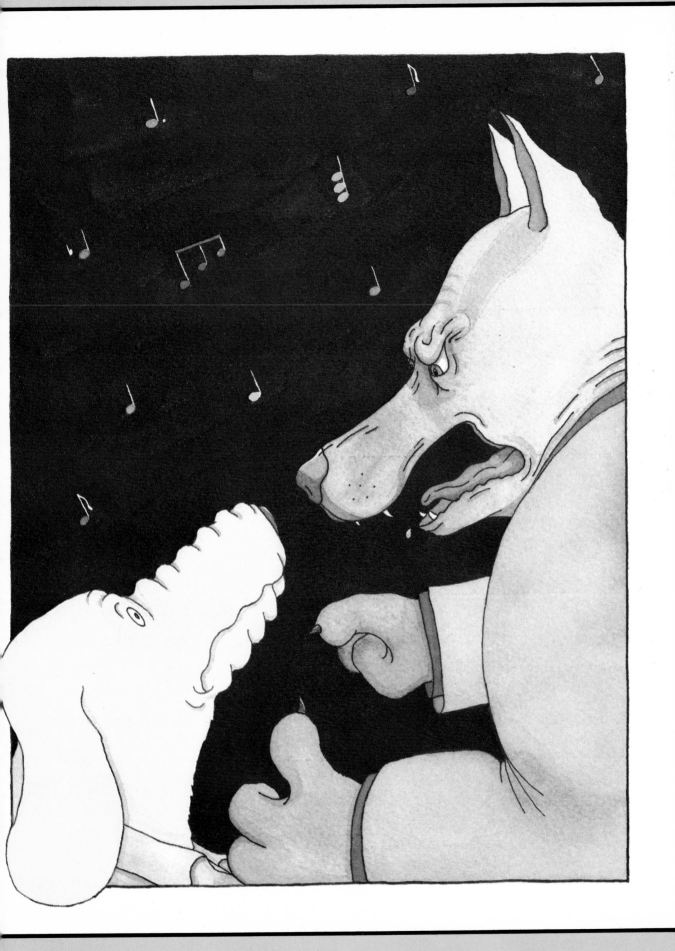

Down and out, Hector walked the streets, wandering aimlessly. Finally he collapsed in a corner, resigned to a life of loneliness and sorrow. "What has become of me?" he sighed.

Bleary-eyed, Hector played a sad, old blues tune.

Hector lost himself in the music. He closed his
eyes and played a beautiful Bach toccata. When he had
finished, standing before him was a crowd tossing
money and cheering, "Bravo! Bravo!"

Hector bowed gratefully and then played a
Gershwin tune, a little Duke Ellington ditty, and ended
with an original composition. The crowd loved it!

Suddenly a figure streaked forward, shouting,
"I am a musical talent agent. Sign here and you will
perform at Canine Hall tonight!"

That evening Hector received a standing ovation from the packed house. "My nose and I are back on top," he thought, "but this time life will be different."

After the show, the lovely opera singer, Miss Lilly deLight (who was starring next-door as Brümhilda in "Die Zaubernüsse") visited Hector in his dressing room to congratulate him. It was love at first sight.

Once again Hector was an overnight sensation. But he and Lilly left the city and made most of their music in the mountains.

The End

Behind the Scenes

Introduction

Miss Piggy, Kermit or Morris the Cat may come to mind first, but animals share our world in many different ways. Some animals we know very well—they are our pets. Others we can read about in books—like Hector in *Hector, the Accordion-nosed Dog*— or see at the zoo. And there are even animals that live only in our dreams—a unicorn is an imaginary animal.

Do You Have A Favorite Animal? Is It Your Pet?

A dog is a great pet because it can be with you so much of the time. Dogs love their owners, so long as their owners love them. Your dog can become a good friend who plays when you want to play and who rests by your side when you are tired. A dog around the house is also good for the whole family. Barking scares away burglars and with a keen sense of smell a dog can alert a sleeping family to smoke or fire in the house.

It takes time to get to know a cat. Cats like to sit and think deep thoughts and sometimes go on hunts without you. Their games are often played alone. But if a cat loves you and sits on your shoulder and purrs, then you know you are truly loved.

Fish have feelings, too. They don't laugh or cry, but they are sensitive to heat and cold and light and dark and the kind of water they swim in. They *feel* the smallest difference in the *aquarium* (say: uh-**kware-ee-um**). There are forty thousand kinds of fish in the world. Studying them can begin in your own little tank. Did you know, for example, that fish see colors, but that cats and dogs cannot? And many fish, known

as *tropical fish*, are very brightly colored. They are interesting to watch and care for as pets.

Birds are a great favorite with many people. No matter what kind of bird you get, you will find they eat very little, they need almost no exercise and, most important of all, each bird has a personality all its own. Some can learn to talk. Some learn to sing. Some even make up their own songs. Bird pets can learn tricks and will perch happily on your shoulder for hours.

Turtles make good pets, too. To keep a turtle you have to have a *terrarium* (say: tuh-**rare**-ee-um) filled with dirt and one or two "climbing" rocks. A bowl sunk in on one side will make a pond for your turtle. Treat a turtle well and it can be a fascinating animal to own. Turtles have good memories and sharp eyesight. If you knock gently on its terrarium before you feed it every day, it will learn to come to the knocking sound exactly as if you called its name.

If you can't resist soft, fuzzy creatures that talk in squeaks and like cuddling, choose a guinea pig for a pet. They are gentle animals. If you keep a male and a female, you will be able to watch guinea pig family life, too. A guinea pig pen should be about a yard square with a wire top that can be opened and wire mesh floors. This way, guinea pigs can get plenty of air and light. Feeding is easy, inexpensive and fun. They love carrot tops, lettuce leaves and dandelion greens. But pet shops also sell a nutritious mixture for your guinea pigs. At supper time, your pets will squeak with delight—they are very enthusiastic diners.

Hamsters are friendly creatures that will beg for petting. They are soft and very tiny. In the wild, hamsters are hoarders of food which they store in underground burrows. They carry food in their large cheeks. Even in the cage you build for them, you can watch your pet hamster take more food than it can eat and store it away in the corners of the cage for nibbling on later. Hamsters can be great fun to play with—but be gentle, they're little animals.

Being a good pet owner is very important. Your pet gives you pleasure and fun. You must give your pet care and protection in return. To be a good pet owner, watch for signs of illness in your pet so that a *veterinarian* (say: vet-er-in-**air**-ee-en), a doctor for animals, can be called if necessary. Your pet also counts on you to take care of it when you travel. In a car you should remember to open the window to let in air if you leave your pet alone. In the summer, a car may get too hot for your pet, so be sure to make plans to keep your pet healthy and happy. And don't forget to offer your pet water at every stop you make. If you can't keep your pet, find a new, happy home for it.

Some people have kept wild animals as pets — chipmunks, raccoons, deer. Wild animals are poor pets. You cannot tame a wild animal, and you should not deprive it of its natural wild life. There is a strong instinct in wild animals to fear and distrust people. It is a dangerous practice to keep wild animals.

Homemade Dog Biscuits

You can make biscuits for your dog easily at home. But be sure to ask Mom or Dad before you get started—they should help you with the measurements and an adult should definitely help with the oven.

Ingredients:

¾ cup wheat germ
1 cup rolled oats (not the instant kind)
¼ cup whole wheat flour
2 eggs, beaten together

3 tablespoons molasses
¼ cup milk
¼ cup salad oil

Turn on oven to 350.°

In a big bowl, combine all the ingredients. Stir well with a wooden spoon or mix with your (clean) hands.

Lightly grease a baking sheet, then drop mixture by spoonfuls onto the sheet, leaving a little space between each biscuit.

Bake at 350° for 15 minutes, then turn off oven and leave biscuits in the oven until they're cool and crisp.

Remove cooled treats and store in a tightly-covered tin. Extras can be stored in the freezer, just remember to take them out a few hours before feeding them to your dog.

And last but not least: clean up!

Dream Animals

Imaginary animals, on the other hand, need no work at all. They do not walk the earth or breathe air. They live in *myths* and *legends* only. Myths and legends are fantastic stories made up to explain strange, real things that people cannot understand.

A unicorn, for example, is only a mythical creature. It appears often in the art of the Middle Ages (a thousand years ago) in Europe. Having the head and body of a horse, the legs of a deer, and the tail of a lion, the unicorn is named for the one horn coming out of its head. Unicorns symbolize purity and meekness. People believed that the horn contained a special medicine to protect against poisons. Today it is believed that the unicorn legend started with stories about seeing a rhinoceros, a very different animal to be sure.

rhinoceros

unicorn

The Loch Ness Monster lives in Loch Ness (*loch* is the Scottish word for lake) in Northern Scotland. The local Scottish people call it "Nessie." If it exists, "Nessie" certainly avoids people. People claim this creature has flippers, one or two humps and a long slender neck.

A creature thought to be more like a human is Big Foot, said to live in America's Pacific Northwest and Western Canada. Canadians call him Sasquatch. Hundreds of people have reported seeing Big Foot or his

footprints. They describe a creature almost eight feet tall, weighing more than 500 pounds. Like an ape, Big Foot has thick fur, long arms, powerful shoulders and a short neck. He supposedly walks like a man. Most scientists don't accept the photos or footprints of Big Foot as proof of his existence. They believe Big Foot is a hoax, or a case of mistaken identity and wishful thinking.

Who—Or What—Is It?

On the other hand, there are real animals that are also mistakenly named. The Komodo dragon, for example, is not a dragon at all. It is the largest living lizard—and lives on the island of Komodo near Indonesia. When it opens its wide red mouth, the Komodo dragon shows rows of teeth like a saw. It hunts animals during the day and digs a cave with its strong claws to hide in at night.

Komodo dragon

Gila (say: **hee**- lah) monsters are not monsters either, but large colorful lizards of the desert Southwest and Mexico. It grows to about eighteen inches in length. The stout body, broad head and stumpy tail have areas of black, brown, and orange or salmon on them. Fat is stored in its thick tail and the Gila monster can live for months without eating. It comes out at night in the desert to find bird and reptile eggs and small animals for dinner. The Gila monster's strong legs let it move with its tail and body off the hot desert earth.

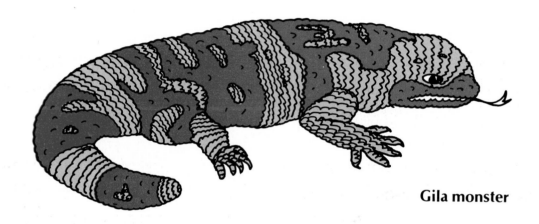

Gila monster

So You Want to Work with Animals?

If you like animals, why not think about working with them? Farming is an important job in our country. There are small, family farms owned by a single family. Parents and children work together to keep the farm going. If you lived on this kind of farm, you would probably wear boots every day after school, because no matter what the season there would be chores to do. And chores are boot work — they are hard, heavy and dirty. You would raise livestock — pigs, cattle, maybe sheep. And grow all the food these animals eat — corn, oats, hay. Some farms raise vegetables and *livestock*, or animals, too.

Once small farms like this fed the whole nation. But as the nation grew, so did its food needs. Now big corporations run giant farms to produce much of the food we eat.

Yet small farms and corporate farms that specialize in one product may exist side by side. Both may raise cows for our dairy products—milk, cheese, yogurt—or cattle, pigs or sheep for the meat on our tables. Poultry farms—chickens, ducks, geese, turkeys—can also be small or so large that factories are built on them to speed production.

Breeding is an important part of raising animals. A farmer who cares about the improvement of his or her animals selects the best ones to reproduce their breed. For example, a chicken should have good egg-laying ability or be plump. In a cow, a farmer might look for milk-producing talent. These are special qualities a farmer would want to keep in a herd. The result of such breeding is a future of finer animals.

Raising show animals is also a good business for those who love animals. Top quality animals compete for prizes in shows around the country. Dog shows, cat shows and horse shows are the most common. There are also events for farm animals. If your animal wins a prize, it becomes more valuable as the parent of a pup, a kitten or a colt.

Showing also involves training your animal to behave well in the show ring, standing properly, walking and performing well for the judges. If you enjoy being with horses, you might want to learn how to groom and take care of them at a nearby stable. A show animal, however, is more than a pet. Show animals can be valuable, and they take a lot of work to keep up a career in the center ring.

Circus Animals

Who wouldn't enjoy working with circus animals? You can be a performer or an animal trainer. You might even want to manage your own circus someday.

The lion tamer works hard to teach the lions and tigers how to do tricks. A tamer is never rough with the animals. This trainer knows that patience and gentleness get better results than bullying.

A bareback rider uses special horses. They must have wide backs, be gentle, and have a good trotting speed. The riders put a sticky substance called *rosin* on the horse's back. This keeps the riders' hands and feet from slipping. Even then, it isn't easy to somersault from a trampoline onto a moving horse's back!

Small circuses have once again become popular recently in the U.S. More like the circuses in Europe, the animal acts are charming in these smaller circuses. They are not scary, just fun. Clowns and acrobats are important in small circuses. And sometimes, bears do folk dances with one another.

The Big Apple Circus is one of the most successful of these smaller one-ring circuses. The home of the Big Apple Circus is New York City (also known as "The Big Apple"). Is there a circus near your home?

Behind the Scenes

Save The Animals

If you came home from school one sunny day and your home was gone, or if your mother gave you a dinner of buttered shoelaces, you would be very confused. And so it is with certain animals. Their homes are changing or disappearing, or they are hunted out of them, or their food supply is depleted or made unclean. If these animals cannot get used to their new environments, which is called *adapting*, they will not be able to survive at all. Animals facing this situation are called *endangered*.

In the case of seals and sea lions, they have been hunted almost to *extinction* in certain places. Extinction, or dying out, means the total loss of that animal from the world. Seal fur is prized, and hunters often kill more animals than is legal. Oil and chemicals in the waters off California cause reproductive problems in the marine animals who live there. And no baby animals, or course, means no future for this species. The only place seals are found in great numbers is Antarctica. Few humans live at the South Pole and few sail there to hunt.

Big cats, such as leopards, cheetahs and lions, are endangered in several ways. Not only are they hunted for their beautiful furs, but they are also hunted as trophies by sportsmen. In the United States there are two wild cats on the endangered list — the Florida panther and the cougar. Both

Panther

of them suffer from overhunting. In many cases, big cats are simply losing their home territory to the changing needs of people. Farms and ranches spring up in their backyards. Cities spread to their doorsteps. They are forced to move where food may be less available, if available at all.

One of the most threatened animals in this country is the eagle. Ranchers claim that eagles kill lambs and calfs, and so some ranchers shoot or poison the birds. Another problem eagles face is that their food sources, small animals and fish, are also dying out. Eagles do not have a secure future any longer. By being named an endangered species, eagles are protected and encouraged to grow in number and strength.

People who care about endangered animals and birds are called *conservationists*. They are trying to save—or conserve—all wildlife. One of the main ways to do this is to set up special "safe environments" or wildlife preserves where animals are protected by law.

There are over three hundred wildlife preserves in this country. For the most part they are open only to scientists or those with a special interest in seeing wildlife in its natural state. These preserves allow animals to live and breed without the often harmful interference of humans, cars, pollution, hunters and other threats to their future.

47

Our National Parks

National parks, on the other hand, are open to anyone and everyone. Yellowstone National Park in Wyoming became, in 1872, America's— and the world's—first national wilderness park. Here the mountains, valleys, rivers, and all the animals natural to this environment, are offered to you as a living museum. Wildlife is protected here. Yellowstone Park became so popular that hundreds more like it were established around the country. From the Crab Orchard Refuge in Illinois to the Everglades in Florida to the cliffs of Yosemite in California, there are national parks open to you and your family.

The National Wildlife Refuge System operates refuges totalling 28 million acres. The System has a very specific aim. It manages migratory birds, protects endangered species and offers Americans enjoyment of wildlife resources. If you visit a wildlife refuge, expect stricter guidelines on your visit than in a National Park. National Refuges operate as giant research projects and the public is welcomed to *observe* but *not to disturb* the natural settings.

There are many opportunities for working in the field of conservation. People are needed to count the animals in certain populations and to study the lives of individual species. Other people study how the public feels about wildlife and what they prefer in conservation. State and federal agencies need administrators to hold legal responsibility for wildlife. Some positions involve improving the living conditions of animals, arranging for hunting seasons, controlling pests, and raising animals on game farms. Others teach the public about conservation, advise courts of wildlife laws, enforce game laws and train conservation workers.

In your community there may be agencies or groups that can use your help in local conservation. Or you may want to join a group of "birders" (or birdwatchers), people who enjoy watching, identifying, keeping track of, and learning from birds.

Here is a map of the United States showing where the National Parks mentioned above are located. Which is the closest to you?

Yellowstone National Park

Crab Orchard Refuge

Yosemite National Park

Everglades National Park

Activities

Transformation

Hector was very proud of his nose. Yet when it changed, he lost heart. How would you feel if you changed? Give it a try with a mask—paper mask. Here's how.

1. Cut a circle on sturdy paper or cardboard.
2. Cut holes for your eyes and mouth.
3. Draw any face you choose on the mask. A scary mask would be fun. Or an animal face.
4. Glue or tape a Popsicle stick to the bottom of the mask for a handle. You can add paper ears, yarn hair, anything you want to make your mask special.

Now you're ready to try a *papier-maché* mask. Papier-maché is a French word that means "mashed paper." This kind of mask takes longer to make, but it lasts longer too. Just follow these easy steps.

1. Tear newspaper into strips. (Make sure Mom and Dad are finished reading it, first!)
2. Make a paste of flour and water. (Add the water slowly. You want the paste to look like mashed potatoes, not too soupy.)
3. Dip the strips of paper into the paste.
4. Place one layer of pasted strips on the inside of a *colander* (a drain bowl with holes in it).
5. Add several layers of pasted strips.
6. Let it dry one or two days.
7. Gently poke the dry papier-maché free of the colander through the holes in the bottom.

8. Cut out holes for your eyes, nose and mouth.
9. Paint a face in bright colors on your mask.
10. Make two small holes on the sides of your mask (where the ears would be). Knot an 8-inch string in each. To wear your mask, just tie the strings behind your head.

Animal Stationery

Send goat notes to your pals. Give paper tigers that growl out greetings. Use giraffes to say thanks. Make this animal stationery by tracing these animals on sturdy paper and then coloring them. Put flowers on your elephants. Hearts on your fish. Go wild!

What A Comic!

Make up jokes—about your teacher, about your pet, about TV characters—and then try telling them to your friends and family. The way you tell a joke is almost as important as the joke itself, so practice your timing. Did you ever notice how LeVar Burton, when he tells a joke on "Reading Rainbow," pauses for effect? When you are ready to try out your act, invite some friends from your neighborhood. Don't just let them judge you, but you judge them, too. What kind of jokes do

they like—one-liners or long stories? Jokes that need a physical movement—a hop or a clap or a fall—are called slapstick. Does your audience enjoy slapstick? Do they *heckle* you? Heckling means talking out loud to the comic, joining the act without an invitation. How well you deal with hecklers can make the difference between being a star and a flop. If some of your friends are comics, too, you can have a laugh-off!

Look Alikes

Did you ever notice how some pet owners grow to look like their pets? Match up the faces below with the pets they most resemble.

Zoo Parade

Here's a word game that puts all the animals you know tail to head in a parade. It stretches as far as your imagination. Start with one animal and then think of another animal whose name begins with the last letter of your first animal's name—Lamb...bear. See? Tail to head. Try it with a friend, and see how many animals you can name.

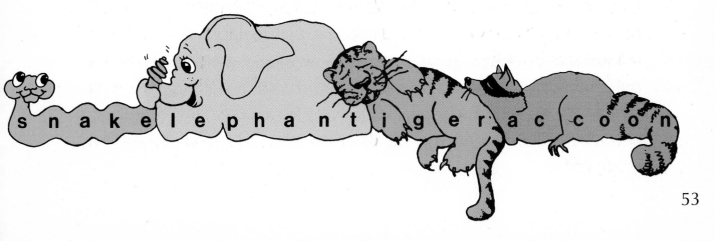

Activities

Barnyard Ballads

Animals make noises we name after how they sound—cheep, bark, meow, moo, baa, cackle, honk, neigh. Say each sound out loud—can you name the animals? Get your friends to join in a barnyard ballad with you—each pick an animal sound, then try singing your favorite song with animal noises rather than words.

griffin

Try to imagine what sound a mythical beast might make. The Loch Ness monster, for instance. Would it hiss like a big snake? Or honk like a giant goose? How about a unicorn? If you were a unicorn, would you neigh like a horse, roar like a lion and baa like a sheep? How about other mythical creatures? A griffin was part lion and part eagle. A centaur was half man and half horse. What sounds would these creatures make?

Make 'Em Laugh

Being a clown is a great job. Clowns make people laugh. You can be a clown too. It's fun to try it yourself.

First, ask your mother for makeup you can use. Left-over Halloween makeup would be perfect. In front of a mirror, draw yourself a clown face. Make big eyebrows, spiky lashes, a red nose, rosy cheeks and lots of freckles. Experiment. You can paint on a happy mouth, turned up at the corners, or a sad mouth, turned down. Then practice making faces — silly faces, sad faces, happy grins. Clowns jump and run and do funny dances, too. They're also famous for *pratfalls*. Pratfalls are funny trips and falls. You flop down easily when you do a pratfall well. Practice on a rug or out on the grass.

Most clowns are *mimes*. A mime is someone who tells a story without words. To mime, you would say "stop" by holding your arm out, palm up. To say no, shake your head from side to side. Make believe you have a dog beside you by leaning over to pat the invisible dog's head. Try telling a simple story in mime.

Bring the circus home with you. With makeup, pratfalls and mime, you can be a clown and make people laugh too.

Birds In Your Neighborhood

Birds travel, or *migrate*, to find food and water when the seasons change. Keep a record of the birds in your neighborhood and if and when they go north and/or south. Your calendar should have places for the name of each bird you want to track, the months of the year, and any notes you want to make about what you see. If you track blue jays, for example, you'll mark one month for when they leave and mark another month for when they return. Check your calendar against bird picture books from the library. Watch carefully again next year to see if the birds follow the same pattern they did this year.

Did You Know...?

- The youngest composer of all time was Mozart. He wrote his first music when he was four years old.

- The biggest live audience for a rock concert was 600,000 people.

- The most successful song writer is Paul McCartney. His song "Yesterday" has been recorded at least 1,186 times.

Animal Chat

We talk a lot about animals even when we're talking about people. Have you ever heard that someone has horse sense? Or someone is a bird brain? And what exactly are dog days? If you have heard these, then you know that horse sense means common sense, since horses are smart enough not to do anything to hurt themselves. A bird's brain is so tiny that calling someone a bird brain means you think that person is stupid. The hottest days of summer are called "the dog days"—after the Dog Star *Sirius,* which rises in the sky during the hottest weeks of the summer. And no one, not even the usually lively dog, has the energy to move in summer's highest heat and humidity.

There are plenty of other animal words we use everyday. Here are some of them. Can you guess where they come from and what they mean?

Stop horsing around! Am I bugging you? I smell something fishy around. Take a cat nap, if you're tired. Are you aping someone?

Activities

Draw Your Pet

Anyone can photograph a pet. Why not do a portrait of yours? Or of a friend's pet? Use colored pencils, crayons or paints. Start by studying your pet. Is the fur soft and fluffy or is it short and wiry? Look at the feet. Are they big or little? Is your pet the same color all over? Be sure to put any spots in the right places! Your pet is different from everyone else's. Your pet portrait can show all the different ways your pet is special.

Make a frame for your portrait. You can make a simple frame with a box and some glue. The box can be white or colored. Just follow these easy steps.

1. Take the cover off a gift box or shoe box. Cut out a space one inch smaller all around than the size of your picture. Example: If your drawing is eight inches by ten inches, the space should measure seven inches by nine inches.
2. Put glue around the edges of the drawing.
3. Place the drawing front down into the top of the cut box.
4. Press the glued edges of the drawing against the edges of the cover.
5. Turn box cover over to see your framed portrait.
6. Put the back on the box and tape the box shut. This portrait box will stand on a desk or a shelf all by itself.

Word Search

Hidden in the maze below are words you've just learned. Do you remember what they mean? The words go across and down. Find them in the maze, then write them on another paper.

UNICORN, ENDANGERED, BIG FOOT, GRIFFIN, CENTAUR, EXTINCT, KOMODO, PRESERVE, WILDLIFE, FARMING, ACCORDION, MIGRATE

E	N	D	A	N	G	E	R	E	D
X	P	F	C	K	R	F	L	M	Y
T	R	L	C	O	I	A	C	I	M
I	E	Y	O	M	F	R	E	G	B
N	S	W	R	O	F	M	N	R	I
C	E	A	D	D	I	I	T	A	G
T	R	Y	I	O	N	N	A	T	F
B	V	O	O	X	S	G	U	E	O
G	E	U	N	I	C	O	R	N	O
W	I	L	D	L	I	F	E	S	T

Activities

A Pig Tale

Count the pig words in this story. There are 10 words—some hard, some easy. Can you find them all?

The football game begins. Nancy has the ball. "Quit hogging that pigskin," her teamate Bobby yells. Nancy charges on anyway, snout down. The other team charges toward her, bristling. Before they meet head on, Nancy looks around and snorts, "I'm alone out here in the mud." Too late, she knows she's made a big mistake. "I've been a real ham," she whines. Just then, Bobby jumps on Nancy's back. "The old piggyback play," he reminds her, and the two of them rush through the other team's line. Under the goal post, Nancy thanks Bobby. "You saved my bacon," she says. Bobby shakes her hand and tells her, "We made the goal together. That's what counts. Being a pig for glory doesn't win for the team."

What's Wrong with These Animals?

You don't have to live on a farm or work in a circus to straighten out these mixed-up animals. Look at the pictures below. Find what doesn't belong on each animal.

Hide and Seek

It's dinner time. Farmer Sandy is out in the barnyard looking for all the animals. Can you help the farmer find a cow, a pig, a sheep, a rooster, a duck, a mouse and two cats named Topsy and Turvy?

Trivia Game

Trivia are facts that may be unimportant but are very interesting. You can make up a game using trivia. Here are some to start you off. Put them on cards. Write the question on one side and the answer on the other. Stump your friends.

1. Q. What song is sung most often?
   A. "Happy Birthday to You."
2. Q. Where is the largest drum in the world?
   A. Disneyland.
3. Q. What is eight feet long and needs six musicians to play it?
   A. The world's largest harmonica.

Activities

Jokes

"Hey, Joe! Did you know that I was teacher's pet?"
"No, Sally. Why's that?"
"She couldn't afford a dog."

What kind of beans will never grow in a garden?
Jelly beans.

"Dad, where were you born?"
"Chicago."
"Where was Mommy born?"
"Dallas."
"And where was I born?"
"Philadelphia."
"Amazing, isn't it, how we three got together?"

Animal Hand Shadows

All you really need to make hand shadows is a light, a wall and your own hands. The brighter the light, the better your animals will be.

Stand or sit with your hands between the light and the wall, and move your fingers to create animals.

Here is a picture to show you the hand movements for a pigeon. Can you make other hand shadows? Use your imagination.

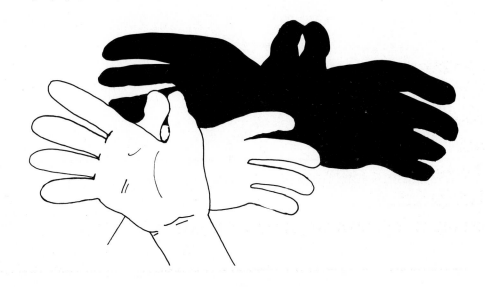

Activities

Play The Accordion

An accordion is a musical instrument that looks like a fan folding and unfolding. You can make one like this.

Cut a piece of construction paper that is six inches wide and twenty-four inches long. Color or paint terrific designs on it—stripes, stars, squares, whatever you like. Then start folding the accordion at one short end. Make one fold and then turn it back against itself and fold it again. Continue until the whole paper has folds like this.

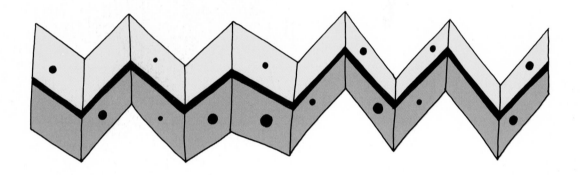

Fan it open and closed. Check out how the design changes as you play your accordion. You'll have to sing along with this silent instrument— what kind of music would your accordion make, if it could?